HOPE'S HORSE

The Mystery of Shadow Ridge

HOPE'S HORSE

The Mystery of Shadow Ridge

Strawberry Shakespeare

Diamond Star Press

LOS ANGELES

HOPE'S HORSE: The Mystery of Shadow Ridge
Second Edition

Second Paperback Edition

ISBN-13: 978-1-7324591-7-5
ISBN-10: 1-73245-917-7

Published by Diamond Star Press

Made in the United States of America

For David Steeves

(1934 – 1965)

Children's Books by Strawberry Shakespeare

NOVELS

Saving Bluestone Belle

Hope's Horse: The Mystery of Shadow Ridge

SHORT STORY COLLECTIONS

The Cloud Horse

SCREENPLAYS

Saving Bluestone Belle

Table of Contents

Chapter One

Goodbye, Grandfather

Hope laid her forehead against the window pane. She watched as a raindrop meandered down the smooth surface of the glass. She thought she had cried every tear she could, but another slipped out from beneath her lashes as she closed her eyes. What would normally have been a beautiful midsummer day was instead rainy, as if honoring her grief by shedding its own tears.

Several days ago, Hope's grandfather passed away in his sleep, and today was his funeral. Her mother and father did their best to comfort her, but in the end, Hope closed herself off in her grandfather's room to say goodbye in her own way.

As much as she loved her parents, Hope and her grandfather had a special bond. People always commented on how she took after him; not because of her shoulder-length brown hair or her deep brown eyes, but because of her natural gift with horses.

As far back as Hope could remember, she had spent the summer days caring for and riding horses on her grandfather's ranch. He had a reputation for being able to tame the wildest mustangs, a talent he passed down to his granddaughter. But earlier that year his health deteriorated. He had to give up his beloved ranch and come to live with Hope and her parents in Allenville.

Grandpa understood her and shared her secrets, but now it was just her and Tango. Hope was waiting for the sky to clear, so she could go to the horse for comfort. Tango was one of the secrets she shared with her grandfather.

Allenville, a small town in the Eastern Sierra Mountains, was known for its herd of wild horses, which the locals viewed as dangerous. The untamed animals could be volatile if confronted by an inexperienced horseman.

As soon as Hope was old enough to be on her own, her parents made it clear she was not to go near the wild horses. She did her best to obey her parents' wishes, but when she happened upon a poacher's trap with a wild mustang ensnared, she had no choice. If she didn't help the horse, he would have perished.

The caramel-colored stallion was so terrified he kicked and flailed, certain to break one of his legs in his panic. Hope approached him without fear. In a low whisper she shushed the mustang, comforting and calming him all at once with the perfect tone and pitch. This was the other secret she had with her grandfather — she was more than a natural with horses. Like her grandfather, she, too, was a horse whisperer. She could communicate with a horse, sense its needs and understand how to reassure it.

The mustang gazed up at her with wild eyes. She continued to softly shush him, careful to remain calm and confident. Finally, he stopped kicking and settled down. He stared at her with unblinking eyes while she cautiously released him from the trap. If he was frightened enough, the moment he sensed freedom, he might have trampled Hope in his urgency to flee. Instead, once he was free, he stood before her trustingly. She reached up and stroked his caramel mane.

"I'm sorry you were trapped," she murmured to the proud mustang, who nuzzled her hand. "We're not all so mean."

From then on, she returned to the woods each afternoon in search of him. She caught glimpses of the horse, but he never drew too close. She named him Tango because he would take a few steps toward her, then back away, and he would do that over and over again, coming a little closer each time. It was as if they were slowly forging a bond through this dance of trust. Calling him 'Tango' just seemed natural to her.

When she confided in her grandfather about the mustang, he offered to teach her how to tame him. At first they practiced with the horses on the ranch. He showed Hope how to run with a horse.

"Hold the reins as tight as you can," he explained, helping his granddaughter grasp the reins. "Now run with the horse, but do your best to keep control." He let go of the reins, leaving Hope clutching them for dear life.

At first the powerful horse dragged her forward. "I can't do it!" she cried with frustration, when each time the horse broke from her grasp.

"Yes, you can," Grandpa assured her. "Talk to the horse. Gain its trust as you run. Let it know, it's not a war, but a team effort." He smiled at that.

Hope tried again. This time, as she ran, she spoke to the horse in a low, calm tone. When the horse started to get jittery, she proclaimed, "We'll do this together." Soon even the wildest horse on her grandfather's ranch responded to Hope's training.

The day finally came when she was ready to try with Tango. Hope and her grandfather went to the edge of the woods where she often saw the mustang. In a short while, they caught a glimpse of him through the branches.

"Come here, Tango," Grandpa commanded.

The horse neighed nervously, but he did draw closer.

"Now, Hope, reach out to him the way I showed you."

Hope offered her hand, palm up to the majestic horse. At the same time she hummed a low, vibrating tone.

Tango seemed intrigued by the sound. When Hope reached up to stroke his mane, he allowed it. But when she tried to loop a lead around his neck, he bucked up on his hind legs. Then he raced off into the woods.

Hope had been very upset. "I can't do it," she said, growling with frustration.

"Yes, you can," Grandpa replied.

Over the next few weeks they returned each day to the same spot in the woods. Soon Tango would come to Hope when she called him. He let her stroke his mane. He even let her rest her head against his strong shoulders. When she thought he was ready, she again tried to slip the lead around his neck.

This time, Tango stood perfectly still. Together they walked out of the woods and onto her grandfather's property.

Hope felt confident at first. "Let's do it," she said to her grandfather as they both gripped the reins, preparing to run Tango.

The mustang bucked and yanked his head against the restraints. "Hold tightly," Grandpa advised.

"It's okay," Hope whispered to the stallion.

Goodbye, Grandfather

The moment her grandfather let go of the reins, Tango lunged forward, knocking her to the ground. Hope tried to release the reins, but they were wrapped tightly around her wrist. As the horse dragged her across the dusty ground, her grandfather chased after them and tried to grab the reins, terrified Hope would be trampled.

Chapter Two

A Lesson in Trust

Hope forgot to be confident as Tango raced around the ring. She forgot the tone she could hum to soothe the wild horse. All she felt was the pain of the reins cutting into her wrist.

"Tango, please!" she screamed. The mustang thrust his head to the side, jerking Hope across the ground and nearly dragging her beneath his powerful hooves. When her eyes, wild with fear, met his, the untamed horse suddenly stopped. It was as if he recognized within her the same terror he had once experienced.

Hope's grandfather crept up slowly, afraid a sudden move might spook the horse. He unwound the reins from her wrist and pulled her to safety. The whole time Tango did not move a muscle.

"Why did he stop?" Hope asked when she was safely out of the ring.

Her grandfather smiled as he cleaned and bandaged her wrist. "Because he saw you for who you are, just as you saw him for who he is. Animals and people are not so different; that understanding is the real secret of a horse whisperer."

He glanced over at Tango who was dashing around the ring again, bucking and whinnying as he shook his caramel mane. "It'll take time, Hope, but one day he'll even let you ride him."

It had taken time, almost a year in fact. When Hope mounted him and was not thrown, she was amazed. The two took off together, and from that day on, when she stood at the edge of the woods and called for him, Tango always appeared.

As if responding to her memories, the clouds parted, revealing the brilliant warmth of the midsummer sun. Streams of sunlight glistened in the drops of rain that had collected on the glass, and she couldn't help but smile at the beauty of it. It seemed like Grandpa was telling her he would be with her, no matter what. Though she was still sad he had passed, she felt a little better, knowing he watched over her and Tango, and all of the Eastern Sierras. With a parting smile to the sunlight, Hope left her grandfather's room.

She told her parents she was going for a walk, but as soon as she stepped out the front door, she took off running. She ran all the way to the trail that led to the edge of the woods. Once there she stopped and peered through the trees. She glanced over her shoulder to make sure no one was following her. When she was satisfied she was alone, she whistled for Tango.

In the distance she heard a neigh calling back to her, followed by hoofbeats that seemed to mimic the pace of her heart.

When Tango burst through the trees, with his caramel mane billowing in the wind, Hope felt a sense of relief. She laid her head against his muscular shoulder and sighed. "It's just us now, Tango." Then she pulled herself up onto his back and patted the top of his head. He whinnied happily.

They started out at a walk and slowly sped up as the trail wound higher on the mountain. The trees towering above them created a canopy that shaded them from the bright summer sun. Now and then some of the raindrops that still clung to the leaves, slid down and fell, striking Hope and Tango. The girl smiled sadly to herself because it seemed as if the mountains were grieving too.

Normally Hope and Tango would explore the woods and meadows near her home, but today she needed to feel the wind in her hair, she needed to remember the rides she and her grandfather took. He taught her to move with the horse, to feel confident as its powerful legs raced beneath her.

She encouraged Tango to continue up the trail until they crossed into a part of the mountain she had never visited before. Hope knew she should turn back to more familiar territory, but her heart was pounding, and she couldn't help smiling. It was the first time she felt good since her grandfather's passing.

Throwing caution to the wind, Hope leaned forward on Tango and whispered beside his ear, "Let's see what secrets this part of the mountain is hiding."

Hope normally followed the rules to the letter, except when it came to Tango, of course. However, for once, she wanted to be as wild as the mustang, and just as free. She imagined she was as lithe and fast as the horse she rode. She knew that if she closed her eyes, Tango's legs would be hers, moving swiftly, each hoof hitting the ground hard. Her hair would be his mane, flowing in the wind. She trusted Tango so much that she was able to let her eyes fall closed for a split second and savor the feel of the wind against her skin.

"Hey!" a booming voice hollered. She was startled, and Tango was spooked. He began to panic, but Hope soothed him, offering a low reassuring tone beside his ear. The voice belonged to a man who burst out of the cover of thick trees. Only then did she notice a house beyond the trees. She had accidentally ridden onto someone's property, and people who lived on the mountain took trespassing seriously.

Fearfully, she guided Tango away from the land they wandered onto, but the horse had a mind of his own. He neighed loudly at the man who approached them.

"Shh, Tango," Hope pleaded. "We're not supposed to be here!"

Chapter Three

The Man on the Mountain

The old man was grizzled and unkempt. His eyes were as wild as Tango's had been when she first found him. Waving a rifle, he shouted, "This is private property! Get off my land!"

Hope coaxed Tango into pacing back a few steps as the man stormed closer, his two mangy dogs at his heels, snarling and barking.

"I'm sorry sir, I didn't realize," Hope said politely. "We were out for a ride and lost track of our direction."

The old man squinted up at the girl and sneered, "Are you even old enough to ride a horse?"

Hope thought he was awfully rude and definitely mean. Suddenly she knew who he must be. There were stories around town about an old recluse. He was rarely ever seen, but when he was, he was never forgotten. No one even knew his name; they just called him "the man on the mountain."

Hope felt a little afraid and wondered what he might do if he grew any angrier. His face was red and his eyes were wide beneath bushy white eyebrows. The dogs growled at her and Tango, teeth bared, while the old man gestured to them to stand down.

"Yes, sir," she answered gently. She spoke to him in the same calm, confident manner she used to soothe the wild horses. "I'm sorry we bothered you." With that she clucked her tongue and turned Tango around.

"Sorry?" the man bellowed, as he and the dogs chased after her. The old man raised his fist and shook it in the air. "You and your horse come trampling onto my land, making a ruckus, and all you have to say is sorry?" His voice was graveled with age and heavy with bitterness.

Glancing back over her shoulder, Hope noticed that the man had cocked the rifle, while the salivating dogs ran in circles, barking loudly. She knew Tango was on the verge of bolting, no matter how much soothing she did.

"Let's go, Tango!" she instructed the horse, and he did not need any more encouragement. He burst into action, carrying Hope swiftly back into the woods. She could still hear the old man shouting in the distance about trespassers and the damage they cause.

At first she was livid that this man would even think to threaten her and her horse. Then, perhaps because of his age, he made her think of her grandfather. She wondered what could have happened in the man's life to make him so miserable. To her surprise, she began to feel sympathy for him. Maybe someone treated him poorly in the past and it caused him to become cranky and violent. Her grandfather once explained to her that when training a horse, you had to think about more than just the animal standing in front of you. Often a horse, especially one that was rescued, had been neglected or abused.

While some trainers believed in demonstrating dominance to break a horse, her grandfather disagreed. "The key is offering them exactly what they need," he explained as he calmed a wild stallion, "someone they can trust."

Hope frowned as she and Tango headed back to the edge of the woods. The man must have gone through most of his life with no one he could trust; it made her feel sad for him.

When she and Tango reached the edge of the woods, she slid off his back and led him to a small pond so he could drink. She had not ridden him that fast in quite some time. His coat glistened with a sheen of sweat as she stroked it. She couldn't help feeling lucky she had so many people in her life she could trust; she had her grandfather, even if he was gone, and her mother and father. Best of all, she had Tango, who was her best friend.

Although Hope had started the day feeling terrible about the loss of her grandfather, after she said goodbye to Tango and walked out of the woods, she found herself feeling grateful she had him to love in the first place. Her entire walk home consisted of thoughts and memories of her grandfather. He gave her a precious gift—a window into the lives and world of horses. It was a world where she felt the most comfortable. While her friends at school were joining clubs and thinking about fashion, she found her refuge in the horses she cared for and the mustang she called a friend.

As the sun began to set, the last remaining clouds of the summer rain painted beautiful colors in the fading light. She thought about the man whose land she had trespassed on. Did he ever notice such beauty in the world around him?

At home, Hope's mother had prepared a light supper of soup and vegetables. The girl sat down at the table and smiled at her parents. Her mother smiled back, relieved to see her daughter was not as sad as she had been earlier.

"I know how hard this must be," her mother said gently.

Hope lifted her dark brown eyes to her mother, who shared the same shade. "It's okay, Mom," she said in a soft voice. "I miss him, but he'll never really be gone."

Her father smiled at his daughter's wise words. For a twelve-year-old, Hope's maturity and understanding never ceased to amaze her parents, who were very proud of their daughter.

Hope felt a twinge of guilt at the pride she saw in her father's eyes. She wondered if he would feel so proud if he knew that, despite her parents' warnings, she had tamed a wild mustang and was off riding him that very afternoon. Maybe one day she would tell them the truth. But today she had to say goodbye to her grandfather; if her mother and father found out about Tango, she feared she would be forced to say goodbye to him as well. Hope simply could not take that risk. As much as it bothered her not to tell her parents the truth, Tango was worth it.

As she drifted off to sleep, she remembered the man on the mountain and hoped he would not get her in trouble by reporting her trespassing.

Chapter Four

On the Run

The next day Hope woke up with one thought on her mind. She dressed quickly and snatched an apple from the bowl of fruit on the kitchen counter. After leaving her parents a note saying she would be back in a few hours, she hurried out the front door.

The sky was pale blue and the air crisp and clear. With the apple tucked into her pocket, she ran toward the woods. She knew the path so well, she could allow her mind to slip away and her body would automatically find its way there. Her thoughts kept drifting back to the man on the mountain. She had a nagging feeling that, despite his gruff exterior, there was something intriguing about him.

When she reached the edge of the woods and whistled for Tango, she heard his hooves striking the ground before she saw him. Greeting him with a smile, she offered him the apple. As she stroked his caramel-colored coat, she noticed he was getting thinner. She worried about him being in the wild without shelter or a regular supply of food. With all of her heart, she wished she could find a way to board him. It was far too expensive, she knew, and her parents would be livid if they discovered the secret she kept.

"I promise to bring more tomorrow," she murmured to the horse, after he devoured his treat. The available food for the wild horses was diminishing, and the poachers had driven many of them away from their usual grazing areas.

Tango shook his mane and neighed, his eyes shining with deep affection for Hope. He ducked his head, inviting her to climb on for a ride.

Hope grinned and hopped onto Tango's back. Soon they were off at full speed, tearing along the trail into the woods. Hope did not have to guide Tango. He knew these woods better than she did; every turn he took led them further along the path. The leaves on the trees were brushed aside as they passed, and the small forest creatures scampered out of sight, clearing the way for the horse and his rider.

Hope was so happy she almost didn't notice the change in Tango. It was not until his pace quickened and his movements became jerky that she realized he was afraid. She glanced around at the scenery whizzing by her. "What is it?" she asked. Although she didn't see anything unusual, she could sense Tango's fear.

His speed increased to the point that Hope felt afraid. She leaned over and wrapped her arms around Tango's neck to steady herself on his back. "Slow down!" she pleaded.

The horse flared his nostrils and twisted his head from side to side, as if he felt surrounded by danger.

Then Hope heard it; the hooves of other horses fleeing. Harsh voices drifted by her ears, their words too muffled to understand, but their intentions revealed in the way they barked at one another.

"Poachers!" Hope hissed as she tightened her grasp on Tango and closed her eyes. She knew that when Tango was afraid he would run faster than any horse she had ever seen. If she wasn't careful, she might fall and get hurt. But there was no way to stop him, now that the wild terror had spread through him.

In the distance, she heard the voices again. This time she could make out a few words.

"We got two today," a masculine voice crowed.

"Not the one I want," another deeper voice replied. "But I'll get him." His laughter carried through the woods as if it were chasing Hope and Tango. "That wild beast will belong to me."

Listening to them, Hope's heart raced. Instinctively, she knew the man was talking about Tango. If the poachers spotted them, who knew what they would do to her in order to get to her horse.

Hope and Tango broke off the smooth path and were now on fairly rocky terrain, with branches of trees close enough to scratch Hope's skin and tear her clothing. She buried her head in Tango's mane and hoped they would make it to safety before the men discovered them.

Tango was breathing hard, and she could feel the pounding of his heart. When he finally began to slow, Hope knew that it wasn't because they were out of danger, but because he was exhausted.

She lifted her head from his mane as he settled into a walk. They were in a part of the woods she had never visited before. In fact, she had no idea which direction would take her home. But as nervous as she was about being lost, her main concern was the poachers. Was this where they did their hunting?

"Shh," she murmured to Tango in a low, soothing tone. She stroked his strong shoulders and hummed with the special vibration her grandfather had taught her.

"It speaks to their souls, not just their minds," Grandpa had explained. "If you can find the right vibration, the right tone, you can calm any horse." He had smiled one of his grand, proud smiles. "Once you gain a horse's trust, he will always be your loyal friend."

When Tango began to respond, Hope slid off his back. She was sore from the ride and needed to stretch her legs. She hoped the poachers were long gone.

After walking with Tango for a few minutes, and continuing to reassure and soothe him, she reached a small break in the trees. It was not a natural clearing. She noticed that the branches high up in the trees had been broken and burned, perhaps by a massive lightning strike or a small brush fire. It was hard to tell exactly what had caused it.

A thick, long branch, wide enough to sit on, beckoned to her. She was exhausted from the ride and from the fear she had felt. As she sat down on the branch, something caught her eye. The sun glinted off of a shiny surface, reflecting it back to her. Hope stood and moved toward it. The metallic object was barely visible beneath the dirt that covered it. She crouched down and brushed the dirt away from the metal, wondering what it could possibly be.

Chapter Five

The Discovery

With each swipe of her hand, Hope exposed more of the mysterious metal object. Stunned, the girl sat back on her heels and stared at what she had uncovered. It was definitely part of something much larger. It didn't look modern at all, as if it had been buried on the mountain for a very long time. She wondered where it came from.

Hope pulled out her cell phone and snapped a photo of what she found. Tango stood over her shoulder, as if he was interested as well.

"Did you know this was here?" Hope asked the horse, who only stared back with wisdom in his eyes. Tango had run out of panic, but Hope couldn't help suspect that perhaps he also wanted to show this to her.

She knew the metallic object was important and could hardly wait to learn the story behind it. But then she remembered she was completely lost in the woods and had no idea how to find her way out. With her muscles sore from clinging to Tango, and her mind spinning from the near encounter with the poachers, followed by finding this strange sheet of metal, she leaned against Tango, completely worn out.

"I understand why you ran," Hope told the horse, who softly nuzzled her cheek, "but now I'm not sure how to get home." She glanced around the woods, seeing only a thicket of rocks, trees and brush. Tango had made his own way up the mountain without the convenience of a path.

She climbed onto Tango's back, and, to her surprise, he immediately headed down the mountain. At first she thought he was just wandering, but then she noticed his gait was purposeful. Hope memorized the twists and turns they took so that she would be able to find her way back to the metal object. She listened closely for any sign of the poachers, but all she heard was the chirps of birds and Tango's slow, steady breathing.

When they returned to a familiar path, Hope smiled to herself. "You brought me home, Tango," she murmured as she stroked his mane. Tango quickened his pace with pride and delivered Hope to the edge of the woods. The moment she slid off his back, he bolted, disappearing into the trees. Hope knew he was still edgy about the presence of the poachers.

The girl ran all the way home, eager to show her parents the picture of what she found. On the front porch, she skidded to a stop. If she showed her parents the photograph, they would want to know what she was doing so high up on the mountain, and how she got there. It would have taken hours on foot to travel so far.

Hope stared at the picture on her phone, and felt her stomach tie into knots. The only way she could explain what she found was by confessing to taming and riding Tango.

She was about to tuck her phone back into her pocket, when her grandfather's voice drifted through her mind.

"If you show the horse trust, he will trust you in return. Horses are not much different than people."

Maybe if she trusted her parents to do what was in her best interest, they would trust her in return. Either way, she knew she could not keep the mountain's secret; it did not belong to her. She found the object for a reason, and now she needed to be brave enough to admit her deception to her parents. She only hoped this action would not cause her to lose her best friend.

When she opened the front door, she heard her parents talking in the kitchen. With each step she took, she grew more apprehensive about what their reaction would be.

"I've heard they took five horses already this week," her father said with distress in his voice. "If Dad were alive…" He shook his head as his throat tightened with grief. "I wish there was something we could do."

Her mother moved to speak, but fell silent when she noticed Hope in the doorway. She didn't want her daughter to overhear such frightening talk; although, if the girl did, she might finally understand why they were so strict about her staying off the mountain and away from the wild horses.

"Hope!" her mother said with a smile. "We were wondering where you were off to so early this morning." She reached out her arms for a hug from her daughter.

Hope remained still, her cell phone in one trembling, dirt-covered hand. When she lifted her eyes to her father, he could see the fear within them.

"Hope," he said with sudden concern, "what's wrong?"

Her mother came closer. "Are you hurt?" She surveyed her daughter for any sign of injury.

Tears sprung to Hope's eyes. She realized her parents would never view her in the same way again. They would know she had been lying to them, and their perception of her as an honest person would be forever altered.

As dire as that knowledge was, Hope knew she had to be brave. "I found something," she said in a hushed, wavering voice.

She held out the cell phone to her mother, who took it with a frown. The woman looked at the picture with

31

confusion. "What is it?" she asked, showing the photo to her husband.

"I don't know," he said, studying it with interest. He glanced up at the girl. "Where did you find this?"

Hope swallowed thickly and blinked back tears. "On...on the mountain," she sputtered.

Her parents' expressions changed swiftly at those words. "What do you mean 'on the mountain?'" her mother said with a warning tone.

"Tell us exactly what happened," her father demanded, as he set the phone down on the counter and focused his full attention on his daughter.

Chapter Six

Hope's Confession

Beneath her parent's scrutiny, Hope felt as if she were as tiny as an ant. They were waiting patiently for her answer. With her throat dry and her eyes moist, she forced herself to speak.

"I have a…a horse," she stammered. Before her parents could react, she rushed forward. "He's a wild mustang…I tamed him with Grandpa." She winced as anger surfaced in her parents' expressions. "I ride him on the mountain, and today he got spooked —"

Hope's father lifted one hand in the air, as if to stop her, but once the words started pouring out, she couldn't hold them back.

"—and he ran. When he stopped, we were on a different part of the mountain, and we found this." She pointed to the picture on the phone. "I'm really sorry I lied to you," she added quickly, then dropped her gaze to the floor and braced herself.

She was met with stunned silence.

"I can't begin to tell you how disappointed I am," her father finally said, his voice so soft, it was almost a whisper.

"But we're glad you're okay," her mother inserted, glancing from her husband to her daughter.

"Of course we are," her father said. "Hope, how could you hide this from us?" He took a step toward her, and Hope's chin trembled.

"We set rules for a reason," her mother intoned. "There are poachers on that mountain, and, as you saw today, wild horses are unpredictable. Even when you think you've tamed them, they still have a wild streak." She shook her head and sighed, "Oh, Hope, you really let us down."

Hope frowned and bit into her bottom lip. She felt horrible for deceiving them, but she felt even worse about what her father said next.

"Young lady, you are not to go near the mountain. In fact, you're not to leave this house except for school, until your mother and I say otherwise."

Hope gasped and shook her head. "But Dad, if I don't take food to Tango—" This time when he held up his hand, Hope silenced instantly.

"You violated our trust, and you're going to have to earn it back. You start by obeying us and not going near that horse." He met her eyes directly, and though his expression softened a bit when he noticed her eyes filling up with tears, he knew what he was doing was for his daughter's safety. "Do you understand?" he asked, his own voice shuddering with a mixture of anger and disappointment.

Hope sniffed, determined not to let her tears fall. She forced herself to nod.

When her mother reached out to comfort her, Hope turned away and ran to her room. She slammed the door shut and flung herself across the bed. But even though she was alone, she couldn't cry. She was afraid that if she grieved, she would never see Tango again. The thought of the wild mustang, waiting for her at the edge of the woods, tortured her. How would he ever understand? Would he think she had abandoned him...or forgotten about him? It broke her heart into pieces. As she shoved her head into the pillow, she wondered if she had made the wrong choice by telling her parents the truth.

A short time later, Hope heard a knock on the door. She did not answer at first; but knowing her parents were standing there waiting, she finally sat up. "Come in," she said with a weary voice.

Her father opened the door and stepped inside. He closed the door behind him and sat on the edge of the bed with her phone in his hand. "I spoke with a deputy at the sheriff's office, and they would like us to come in tomorrow." He sought Hope's eyes, which were red and still rimmed with tears.

"I know that you think your mother and I are being cruel, but you are the most important thing in the world to us, and sometimes adults do know better. There's a lot more danger on that mountain than just the wild horses."

With a sigh, he stood up and handed her the phone. "I would like you to come with me tomorrow and show this picture to the sheriff."

Hope nodded, avoiding his eyes. She wanted to tell him about the poachers, but she was already in enough trouble. Even though she didn't agree with her parents' punishment, she couldn't deny that they were right about the danger. She could only hope they would come to realize that Tango was not a danger to her at all; he was her best friend.

After her father left the room, Hope held the phone close to her heart and thought of Tango. If he had not fled when he did, the poachers might have caught them both. She knew that no matter what her parents thought, Tango had run not only because he was afraid, but because he was also trying to protect her.

Chapter Seven

A Piece of History

The next day Hope and her father drove into town to deliver the picture to the sheriff. They rode in silence, both still upset about the day before. Hope was glad her father let her come along, but she was nervous about what the sheriff would say. She wondered if he would be happy with her discovery.

As they drove past the woods, she looked out the passenger side window and sighed. She imagined Tango running out of the woods, galloping beside the car, his long mane whipping in the wind. He was free to do what he pleased, while Hope felt like a prisoner.

The portly Sheriff Saunders greeted them warmly in the front office and then turned them over to an unsmiling Deputy Greene.

The deputy studied the photo. "I can't be sure what this is until we get a closer look." Then he turned to Hope with a frown. "Were you alone up there?"

Hope looked away as her father spoke for her. "Yes, despite the fact that we've explained the danger to her." He shook his head sadly and then added. "She won't be going up there alone again."

Deputy Greene glared at Hope. "I hope not. It's not a safe place for someone your age."

"Yes, sir." she said quietly. Hope felt like she was getting a lecture all over again. She was a little disappointed that the deputy was not more excited about what she had found.

Another deputy walked up to the first and glanced over the man's shoulder at the picture. "Do you think you could show us where this is exactly?" he asked the girl.

Hope saw her father grimace; he had made her promise to stay off the mountain.

"Deputy Jarvis, Mr. Miller and I were just explaining to this young lady the danger of the mountain," Greene said.

Jarvis nodded and flashed a charming smile. "Of course; but we could put together a small search party and have a look together." The object triggered his curiosity, as it was not often they found something on the mountain. Once anything crashed or was buried there, it could be lost for decades. Maybe the sheet of metal in the picture was from an old vehicle or a make-shift shelter of some kind. But if it was a piece of a plane, as he suspected, it could have historical significance.

When Hope's father finally nodded, Deputy Jarvis grinned with anticipation. "I'll run it by the sheriff, and then it'll take a few days to organize a search party." He smiled at Hope as Deputy Greene downloaded the picture to their computer. "We'll be in touch."

Hope spent the next three days in a sullen state of mind. With every passing hour, she thought only of Tango and whether he was safe, or if he might be hungry. Her parents tried to talk to her about it, but Hope had nothing to say.

On the third night, as she was watching the news on television with her parents, there was a story about the poachers.

"It's out of control," a woman from the horse rescue center declared to the reporter. "The mountain terrain makes it nearly impossible to capture these men, and the herds are dwindling. Food is scarce and the poachers are taking advantage of that. They're targeting the only places the horses can find sustenance and setting traps for them."

The woman was visibly upset, and Hope grew angrier with every word she spoke. Finally, the girl jumped up from the couch and swung around to her parents. "Don't you see why I need to check on Tango?" she yelled.

Her parents exchanged a worried glance, but when her mother spoke, her tone was firm. "Hope, I know you care for Tango and think it's your job to keep him safe, but he is a wild horse and can fend for himself. You are a vulnerable young woman, who a poacher could easily hurt." She stood and tried to hug Hope. "Please try to look at it from our side. We're only trying to keep you safe."

Hope pulled away from her mother's embrace and shook her head. No matter how hard she tried to explain, it seemed her parents would never understand.

Lying in bed that night, she considered breaking her parents' trust once again. She could slip out when they were asleep. But she knew that going on the mountain at night would be far too dangerous.

As she grew sleepy, her mind filled with memories of riding through the woods on Tango's back. But this time the trees echoed with the sounds of other horses, neighing from a distance. Their cries were full of fear. They were calling to Tango to help them. Then Tango neighed as well, and Hope realized that perhaps they were all calling to her for help.

What could she possibly do to help? How could one girl stop a group of poachers once and for all?

Chapter Eight

Lost and Found

Hope awoke with a deep sadness. Tendrils of her dream clung to her memory. She could still hear the desperation in the horses' cries.

"Hope?" Her father knocked lightly on the door.

She sat up on the edge of the bed. "Come in," she said morosely.

When he stepped into the room and saw her face, he was troubled by the sorrow in her expression. "Deputy Jarvis called this morning. The search party is ready to go. We're meeting them in an hour." He tried to catch his daughter's eye, hoping the news would cheer her up. She nodded faintly, but offered no other reaction.

After her father left the room, Hope dressed. She no longer cared very much about the metal object, but a surge of enthusiasm did arise within her heart when she thought of the possibility of seeing Tango. By the time she and her father left the house, she was smiling again.

Hope and her father were the first to arrive at the meeting place near the woods. She was tempted to whistle for Tango, but just then, Deputy Greene, Deputy Jarvis and three other deputies appeared.

As she and the group trudged up the trail, she kept hoping that Tango would come bounding over. If he had, she might have been able to show her father how tame he was. But of course, he did not come. There were so many people with her, he was likely spooked.

"How often do you come up this way?" Deputy Greene asked.

Hope cleared her throat and glanced guiltily at her father. "Often," she replied honestly.

The officer nodded as he held back a branch so Hope could walk past. "Have you ever seen anyone else on the mountain?"

Hope froze. She didn't know what to say. She had seen the old man, and she had seen the poachers. If she told him that, her father would be even more furious.

"Uh," she said, forcing a smile, "I don't usually see anyone else." It was not exactly a lie. Most of the time, it was just her and Tango. Deputy Greene studied her as Hope held her breath, expecting more questions.

"Take a look at this!" Deputy Jarvis called out from further up the trail. The interruption saved Hope from the inquisitive deputy, who hurried forward.

When Hope and her father arrived, the men were inspecting the remains of a campsite. "Looks like those poachers were here," one of them commented, pointing to a shell casing on the ground.

Hope's father placed his hands protectively on her shoulders. "How much further is it, Hope?" he asked.

The girl pointed ahead. "Just around the bend," she said in a quiet tone. She knew it upset her father to realize she had been so close to such dangerous men. He started to lecture her, but Deputy Greene cut in.

"And you said you did not see or hear anyone else?" he asked Hope, placing his hand on the butt of his gun and fixing her with a withering stare.

Hope lowered her eyes to the dirt beneath her shoes. She could feel her father's hands tightening on her shoulders. "I was with my horse, Tango. He's a wild mustang," she began. "I guess maybe he sensed the poachers and took off running." She lifted her chin. "He must have been trying to protect me."

"Protect you, by racing off through the woods?" her father retorted. "That's not safe at all, Hope. The horse could have thrown you."

All the men nodded in agreement.

"You took a big risk by being on a wild horse and going this far up the mountain," Greene admonished her. "Show us where the wreckage is," he said gruffly.

When Hope took the lead along the trail, he added, "We'll talk about what you did and didn't see, later."

The girl grimaced at the inference she had more to reveal.

After a few more minutes of walking, Hope pointed out the shiny metal surface, which was nearly covered up by dirt. "There it is," she said with a touch of excitement. Although she was upset, she was still curious about her find.

Deputy Jarvis crouched down and brushed the dirt away from the surface.

"What do you think it is?" Hope asked.

Jarvis was quite interested in historical planes, and he suspected that what he was looking at could be the cockpit of a small plane. "It looks like it might be wreckage from a plane crash, but it's impossible to tell for sure until it's fully recovered." He stood up and scanned the heavy cover of trees surrounding them. "This is Shadow Ridge. No one would have found this for decades, I'm sure, if it had not been for you and your mustang." He flashed a smile at the girl and patted her lightly on the shoulder, while Greene looked on, frowning.

Just then a loud, popping sound shattered the peacefulness of the woods.

"Gunshot!" one of the deputies announced.

Jarvis pulled Hope to the ground. "Stay still and be quiet," he hissed into her ear, as more shots rang out.

Chapter Nine

Two Heroes

Deputy Jarvis stayed with Hope and her father, while the other deputies drew their weapons and fanned out through the woods, seeking the source of the bullets. Hope could only think of Tango and whether he was in the middle of the gunfire.

Her father patted her back. "It's going to be okay, sweetie," he whispered.

Hope nodded, but she was scared, not so much for herself, but for Tango. Then she heard a horrible sound that shook her to the core. It was the sound of a horse snorting fearfully and then squealing defensively. She couldn't tell if it was Tango. A shot rang out in the air, and the horse was suddenly silent.

"No!" Hope cried out, despite the shushing of her father and the officer. Hope wriggled out of her father's grasp and fled. She ignored their calls as she raced through the trees. Soon she could hear their shouts no more, aware only of the wind in her hair and the trail beneath her feet. Her heart slammed against her chest as an image of Tango, hurt, flooded her mind.

She broke through the trees into a clearing. Before she realized it, she was right in the middle of a passel of horses and three men with rifles. The horses were restrained, swaying sleepily in place. Hope froze as she realized what she had done. She backed away, but it was too late. One of the men had spotted her.

"Hey!" he shouted, lifting his rifle. "Where do you think you're going?" The man approached her aggressively. He was tall and muscular, and Hope knew that even if he didn't have a gun, she would have no chance of fighting against him.

He pointed the long barrel of the gun at her and smirked. "Come over here," he said, gesturing with the gun.

The terrified girl raised her hands in the air, wondering what to do. If the poachers knew the deputies were in the woods behind her, they would try to protect themselves by holding onto her. "I...I just got lost," she stammered. "You can let me go. I won't tell anyone."

"She's lost," he called over his shoulder to the two other men, who were watching with their guns raised. "We should just let her go." He laughed and grabbed Hope roughly by the shoulder. "Come on, girl, you should not have been so nosy." He shoved her over to the other two men. Both were also quite large and their weapons just as deadly.

Hope glanced at the horses. They were all wild, but none of them were Tango. She could see a few mares and a colt. Two stallions were tied to the back of a horse trailer, their heads hung low. Hope knew they should have been fighting for their lives; the poachers must have drugged them with something.

The men looked Hope over. "What are we going to do with her, Boss?" one of them asked. His face was grizzled and smudged with dirt. The man standing beside him was clean cut, but his cheeks were bright red with sunburn. Neither seemed troubled by holding a young girl hostage.

"Just worry about the horses," the man in charge said, with a quick glance through the trees. He felt as if he was being watched. "Get them in the trailer, and hurry up about it," he said flatly, his weapon trained on Hope.

Hope watched as each of the beautiful horses was loaded onto the horse trailer. They crammed many more into the van than it was supposed to hold, but the poachers didn't seem to care if they fit or if they were safe.

"Good haul," one of them commented after they loaded the last horse.

A loud, crunching sound came from the woods. "What's that?" the leader hissed, pointing his weapon at the trees. "Is there someone else out there?" he barked at Hope. She winced at the sound of his voice and shrunk from the weapon he pointed at her.

Deputy Greene stepped out of the woods with his weapon lowered.

"Put your weapons down!" he shouted, as the other deputies emerged from the trees behind him.

The leader of the poachers grabbed Hope around the waist and yanked her against him. "Come any closer and she's done for," he threatened, glaring at the officers.

Hope knew that as long as he had her they would not fire on him. But before the officers could respond, a loud squeal carried through the trees, drawing everyone's attention.

Hope knew that squeal, and she knew the wild mustang that burst through the tree line and out into the clearing. He charged so quickly, the poachers surrounding Hope didn't have time to raise their weapons. Bucking and waving his powerful legs wildly in the air, he squealed again. The horses in the trailer, despite being drugged, began to squeal and snort back at Tango. Tango's legs came down on one of the men, while the other dove out of the way.

The man holding onto Hope raised his weapon in the air and pointed it directly at Tango.

"No!" Hope screamed, struggling desperately to free herself from the man's grasp. A shot rang out, and the horses squealed and neighed loudly as Tango's feet hit the earth hard.

Chapter Ten

Revelations

Hope crumpled to the ground in front of Tango, who nickered softly at her. The man, who had held her so tightly, dropped his weapon. He had no choice, with blood pouring from his forearm. He was shot before he had the chance to hurt Tango, who was now nuzzling Hope's cheek.

The deputies rushed in and subdued the men.

"Who fired?" Deputy Greene demanded to know. One of his men pointed across the clearing, in the opposite direction. "The bullet came from over there, sir," he said. As he pointed, a man stepped out of the trees on the other side of the clearing. He knelt down, placed his weapon on the ground and raised his arms in the air.

Hope recognized him immediately. It was the man on the mountain!

Hope felt strong arms lifting her to her feet and encircling her in a crushing embrace. "Oh, Hope, I'm so glad you're okay," her father cried.

She knew a lecture was imminent about running off and ignoring their calls, but in that moment, all she could feel was relief.

Hope reached out to stroke Tango's mane, unable to take her eyes off the old man, who the officers approached cautiously. They ushered him away before she even had a chance to say 'thank you.'

"Dad," Hope said softly as she brushed her hand across Tango's caramel coat, "this is Tango."

Her father frowned, but he reached out and tentatively stroked the mustang's back. It amazed him to see the horse come to his daughter's rescue like that; but he also saw how wild he was. The stallion had nearly trampled one man, and his eyes were still large with fear.

Tango only allowed Hope's father to touch him because she was humming in that low, soothing tone.

"He sure does love you," her father murmured, smiling at the way the horse nuzzled Hope and nickered beside her ear.

On the way home, Hope stared out the window. The further away from the woods they drove, the greater her sorrow grew. She knew the poachers would be under lock and key, and the stolen horses would recover in the nearby rescue center. But Tango had bolted before he could be restrained. Though her heart was heavy, she was secretly glad he had, even if it meant she would never see him again. She knew the wild mustang would never be happy living at a horse rescue.

When they arrived home, Hope went straight to her room. She needed to be alone for a little while to sort through everything that happened.

A few days later, the phone call Hope and her parents had been waiting for finally arrived. They gathered around and switched the phone to speaker so they could hear it together.

"What Hope found was a small plane," Deputy Jarvis said, "and we even managed to recover the serial number. We have some exciting information about it."

Hope and her parents listened closely as the deputy continued.

"It's the remains of a Lockheed T-33 jet that was flown by an Air Force pilot named Don Stevenson back in 1957. The plane crashed in the Sierras while he was on an Air Force mission."

Hope and her father glanced at each other with wide eyes.

"Stevenson survived the crash, but he didn't make it out of the wilderness for another two months. Meanwhile, the plane was never found, not even after dozens of searches." He lowered his voice as he added, "The military thought he was lying about the crash."

Hope shook her head, frowning. "Why would he ever lie about that?"

"It was a different time then," Jarvis said gently. He knew the era well as it had held his interest since he was a young man. "The Cold War was in full force. When Stevenson first appeared, he was hailed as a hero, but when they couldn't find the plane, they suspected him of treason."

Hope gasped, and her father tightened his lips into a grim line. Both knew that was the worst thing a man fighting for his country could be accused of.

"They figured he had sold the plane to the USSR, but they couldn't prove it. He was under a cloud of suspicion and had to resign from the Air Force."

Hope was furious at how this man had been treated so unfairly. It must have been torture for him to be accused of such a terrible crime, the whole time knowing that the plane was somewhere on the mountain.

"Is he still alive?" the girl asked hopefully.

"Yes," Jarvis replied. "It seems he moved here to continue his search and has never left. As a matter of fact, we've arranged a meeting with him tomorrow. If it's okay with your father, we'd like you to come along."

"Me?" Hope exclaimed, shooting a quick glance at her father, who nodded.

"Well, you're the one who found the plane," Jarvis countered, and then added with a touch of mystery, "I think you'll find him very interesting."

After they hung up the phone, Hope could not stop thinking about the pilot, Don Stevenson. She hoped that, despite the many years that had passed, knowing the plane was found would give him some sort of peace.

Chapter Eleven

A Visit with an Old Friend

ope had mixed feelings about meeting Don Stevenson; after all, he must still be angry about what happened to him. Could her discovery of the plane ever heal the years of pain?

"I can't believe he never moved away," Hope murmured as she and Sheriff Saunders drove toward the mountains. She would have moved a thousand miles away from anyone that had treated her so poorly.

The sheriff nodded sadly. "In fact, he spent most of his life searching for that plane. He used to fly back and forth over the Sierras. He even hiked all over the mountain, but he never found it." He frowned and rubbed his chin. "Folks around here acted like he was crazy. I guess we all just assumed he was trying to defend his honor after making a horrible mistake."

Hope became distracted by the road they were taking up the mountain. "He lives on the mountain?" she asked with surprise.

The sheriff nodded. "I guess he never could give up looking."

When they pulled into Mr. Stevenson's driveway, Hope was shocked at the condition of the property. The house itself looked untended, with wood rotting in places. It was set back quite far from the road, and the bushes and trees had overgrown any walkway that might have once led up to the sagging porch.

The sheriff stepped around the car to open her door. Hope hesitantly climbed out. The land looked familiar, but she didn't know why. She didn't recognize the house, yet she felt certain she had been there before. Behind the building, several dogs barked, warning the trespassers to tread carefully.

The sheriff led her up the stairs, offering her his hand to assist her over the broken steps. He banged on the door. After a few moments passed and no one answered, the sheriff tried the doorknob. The door fell open.

"It's Sheriff Saunders!" he called out as he moved into the house.

Hope followed behind him. It took some time for her eyes to adjust to the darkness. It was so bright and sunny outside, yet somehow not an ounce of light managed to get inside the house. As her eyes adjusted, she could see it was clean and neat, but there were no decorations, no personal touches. She frowned at that. She could tell already that whoever lived here was a very sad person.

It seemed as if no one was home, until the sheriff paused beside the open basement door. They could hear scratching sounds coming from below.

"Hello," the sheriff called as he and Hope descended the stairs.

"Who's there?" a man shouted, slamming down the tools he had been using to make a wood carving.

"This is private property!" he hollered as the sheriff reached the bottom of the steps. "You don't have any right to be here!"

"Calm down, sir," the sheriff said. "The door was open, and I've come with good news."

When Hope appeared, the old man became even more irate. "What's she doing here?" he bellowed. Out back, the dogs howled at the sound of their owner shouting.

Hope recognized him right away. It was the man on the mountain! Was it possible that the man she had been feeling sorry for all morning was the same angry old man who had first threatened her and then saved her? After her initial surprise, she realized it made sense. No wonder he was so angry and bitter, after what he had been through. She even felt a twinge of guilt for the way she had thought of him in the past.

"She's here because she found something that belongs to you," the sheriff said. He removed his hat and pressed it to his chest, "Mr. Stevenson, I'm here to inform you that your plane has been found and is being recovered as we speak." He glanced over his shoulder at Hope, "Thanks to this young woman, Hope Miller."

Mr. Stevenson looked stricken as the sheriff's words sunk in. He had searched for years, until one day he had finally given up hope. He met the girl's eyes and realized she couldn't be more than eleven or twelve years old. "You found it?" he queried, his voice wavering.

"Yes."

"Where was it?" he asked brokenly.

"On Shadow Ridge."

"Shadow Ridge," the old man repeated as if in a trance.

Hope nodded and added with sincerity, "I'm sorry you went through so much." Perhaps she had not been the first to treat him poorly, but she had bought into the stories of the frightening old man on the mountain.

Mr. Stevenson's breaths came short and fast at the sheriff's next words. "A representative from the US Air Force will be coming to visit you today. You can expect the media too; this story will be all over the news."

Mr. Stevenson covered his face with his hands to hide his tears. He was certain he must be dreaming. Then he felt Hope's hands on his, gently pulling them away from his face. She smiled into his teary eyes and whispered, "Thank you for saving us."

He pushed her off of him and glowered at the girl. "I saved the horse!" he shouted, his tears replaced by rage. Everything was changing so quickly, and he felt like this young girl had disrupted his life.

Hope backed away from his anger, and the sheriff stepped in front of her. "We'll be on our way," he said sternly. Without another word, they turned and headed up the stairs, but Mr. Stevenson followed close behind to make sure they didn't snoop around.

As Hope and the sheriff left the house, a man in full Air Force regalia was just arriving. Recognizing the man's rank, Mr. Stevenson snapped to attention. The Major lifted his hand to his forehead and greeted Mr. Stevenson with a sharp salute and an abundance of respect.

Mr. Stevenson stood taller than he had in years, pride evident in his expression. He clicked his heels and lifted his hand to his head, returning the salute as if he were twenty-three years old again.

Hope glanced back over her shoulder in time to catch a glimpse of what Don Stevenson must have once been like; a proud, loyal man who would do anything for his country.

Chapter Twelve

In the Spotlight

There was a lot of excitement in Hope's household the next morning. The phone rang repeatedly with news reporters asking for her story. Meanwhile, Hope was preparing for a photo shoot by the local newspaper. Mr. Stevenson would be there too, and while she was thrilled she had made such an important discovery, she was also nervous about seeing him again. It didn't seem to matter to him that she had found his plane. In fact, it had only seemed to make him angrier. Was he so angry that he'd tell her parents she trespassed on his property? The thought of it made her stomach do flip flops.

Although the excitement was a distraction from her grief, Hope could not stop thinking about Tango. She knew there was no chance she would be allowed on the mountain alone again, and certainly not to ride Tango. She worried that he might be hungry, but she was relieved the poachers had been arrested. The mountain was a little safer for the wild horses, and that helped her feel a little better.

Hope's father noticed the sorrow in her expression. "Are you ready for today?" he asked.

"I guess," Hope replied with a forced smile.

"Don't worry, kiddo," her father said lightly, "there's nothing to be shy about."

Hope nodded, as if that were the problem.

When Hope and her parents arrived at the edge of the woods for the photo shoot, the reporter and photographer were already waiting. The girl held her breath, hoping she would have a chance to see Tango.

She almost didn't recognize the man who stood with his back straight and his chin high, fully dressed in uniform. It wasn't until he glowered at the reporter that she realized who he was. "Wow," she murmured to herself in amazement. Then he turned his serious gaze toward her.

"Hello, Mr. Stevenson," Hope said politely.

He stared at the girl and said nothing.

"It's an honor to meet you," her father said with deep respect, offering his hand. He knew that the man before him had served their country, and he was grateful for it.

Mr. Stevenson shook his hand, but he didn't look away from Hope. She couldn't tell if he was angry. Before she could ask, the reporter reappeared, followed by Deputy Jarvis.

"Just want to go over a few things before we start," the smartly dressed newswoman said to Mr. Stevenson.

While the old man was distracted and her father was busy talking to Deputy Jarvis, who was there to detail the history of the story, the girl peered past every leaf and branch, hoping to catch a glimpse of Tango.

"Hope!" her father called, "they're ready to start."

Hope sighed as she looked away from the woods. When she turned around to face the others, she made sure she had a pleasant smile on her face. She wanted everything to go well, to prove to Mr. Stevenson, once and for all, that she didn't mean to cause him any trouble.

While the photographer adjusted his equipment, the reporter caught her eye. "Since we'll discuss the poachers and the scarcity of food for the wild mustangs, I was hoping that Tango might be in a few shots."

Hope's heart leaped at the idea then fell just as quickly. "I'm not sure he'll come with all these people around," she explained, "but I'll try."

The girl walked to the very edge of the woods and whistled loudly and clearly for Tango. In the distance, they could hear hoofbeats approaching, but they could not see the horse. Hope caught a flash of caramel out of the corner of her eye and finally spotted Tango not too far off in the woods.

She whistled again, but Tango snorted at the strangers and danced back nervously. When the photographer tried to snap a picture, the sound made Tango flee into the woods.

"I'm sorry. It's just too much for him," Hope said with a frown. Her heart pounded when she imagined chasing after Tango. If only she could ride him one last time.

Once the interview was underway, Hope answered the reporter's questions politely, while at the same time, her mind was still reeling with thoughts of Tango.

Mr. Stevenson didn't like all the fanfare, but he responded to the woman's questions as clearly as he could. He knew it was the only way his message would get out to everyone that had turned away from him and believed the worst about him.

He stared hard at the newswoman as he spoke his final words. "With the discovery of my plane, now everyone will know that my loyalty has always been, and will always be, dedicated to this wonderful country."

The reporter grinned and gave a thumbs up to the photographer, who snapped his last shots. "This story is going to be a smash!" she exclaimed.

Hope smiled at the newswoman, but it was forced. "Do you think it might do something to help the horses?" she asked.

While Hope and the reporter talked about the lack of food and safety for the horses, Mr. Stevenson studied the woods.

"Such wonderful animals, and the rest of the world has forgotten about them," Hope said sadly. This seemed to get Mr. Stevenson's attention, as he met Hope's eyes for just a moment.

The reporter glanced toward the woods. "Maybe we should call the horse one more time. The story doesn't seem complete without a shot of Hope and Tango."

"If Hope goes to him and rides him back here, maybe he'll feel safe," Deputy Jarvis suggested, drawing looks of displeasure from Hope's parents.

"Hope has already been told she is not allowed to ride that horse anymore," her father stated.

The possibility of riding Tango flooded Hope with excitement. "Oh, please, Dad," she begged. "I promise I'll be careful."

"I'm sure she wouldn't have to ride him far," the reporter added with an ingratiating smile.

Hope's mother nervously scanned the woods around them. "I'm not sure it's a good idea." Even though the poachers had been arrested, she knew there could still be danger beyond the tree line.

"Just one more time, please?" Hope pleaded.

Chapter Thirteen

A Home for Tango

After a few minutes of conversation between themselves and Deputy Jarvis, Hope's parents finally agreed to let her ride Tango out of the woods.

Disappearing into the brush, Hope could barely contain her joy. She whistled for Tango, but at first there was no response, so she moved deeper into the woods. She whistled again and climbed the mountain trail.

Suddenly she heard the hooves of many horses striking the ground. She was high up enough to see the plains that stretched out below her. Her breath caught in her throat as she witnessed at least a dozen horses galloping together. Tango ran at the front of the herd, his caramel-colored mane billowing out behind him.

Hope whistled clearly again. Tango dropped away from the herd and raced to join her. A short while later, the magnificent stallion broke through the trees and trotted up to her.

"Tango!" the girl cried, ecstatic to see her best friend. She stroked his caramel coat, then climbed easily onto his back and rode him back down the trail.

Everyone was quiet as Hope slid off of Tango's back. He eyed the strangers warily and snorted a little, but Hope soothed him with low tones. She pulled an apple out of her pocket, which she had taken with her just in case. As Tango ate the apple, he eyed the photographer, who approached him slowly.

Hope murmured, "It's okay. He won't hurt you."

Once the photographer snapped all of the photos he needed, Hope knew she would have to take leave of her beloved mustang. The horse nuzzled her cheek.

"I love you, Tango," Hope whispered. Then she closed her eyes and softly hummed into the horse's ear, saying goodbye to him in their own special language.

Suddenly, Mr. Stevenson blurted out, "I have room on my property. Maybe I could give Tango a safe place to stay."

His offer silenced everyone. Such generosity from a man with a very gruff nature was quite a surprise. Hope understood it though, because in many ways he was similar to the wild horses. Underneath his crusty exterior, he was a great man that his friends and family had forgotten.

"Would you really?" Hope asked. It thrilled her to think that Tango would be safe.

"On one condition," Mr. Stevenson said sternly. "There's a lot to be done on my property; cleaning, repairing. Taking on a horse would mean a lot of work. You would have to agree to help me or it can't be done."

"Of course!" Hope cried.

"It will be hard work," Mr. Stevenson said sharply with a frown, as if he thought Hope wouldn't be able to do it.

"I can handle it!" Hope insisted. She would gladly work her fingers to the bone to prepare a new home for Tango. Her heart soared at the thought of seeing the horse on a regular basis.

"Then all that's needed is your parents' approval."

Hope turned excitedly to her father, who looked questioningly at his wife.

"Hope did help Dad at his ranch quite often," her father said with a frown.

"But Tango is still a wild horse," she pointed out.

Mr. Stevenson nodded. "He is, but I have never seen a wild horse protect a person, the way he did your daughter."

Hope swallowed thickly as she saw the hesitance in her mother's expression. "Mom," she said in a confident voice, "horses are not so different from people. Sometimes you have to show them a little trust."

Her mother sighed and smiled. "When did you get so wise?" she asked, with a hint of pride in her voice. Then she hugged Hope tightly and agreed to the arrangement.

"Now," Mr. Stevenson said, "we just have to ask Tango."

Over the next few weeks, Hope was at Mr. Stevenson's house as often as possible. It was hard work clearing the overgrown property, but the thought of seeing Tango was all the motivation Hope needed.

Her dedication didn't escape Mr. Stevenson's notice. The girl never complained or asked for help. At first he only spoke to her to assign her tasks. But as the days passed, he would bring her glasses of water and offer small compliments on the progress she had made. Then together they painted the barn and the house. The property was becoming tidy, and the fresh paint brightened it up as if the sun were shining on it once more.

On the afternoon they completed the paddock the old man stood back and observed their handiwork.

Hope could see a sense of pride in his eyes and a brief, peaceful expression flutter across his features.

"Hope, come inside for a minute, I have something for you." It was the first time in years he had invited anyone into his home.

While he went down to the basement, Hope sat down on the couch in the living room. She thought it was strange he had invited her in and wanted to give her something, but she was glad he was finally warming up to her.

As she leaned down to tie her shoe, she noticed the corner of a book sticking out from beneath the couch. She reached down and picked it up. The cover was well-worn, and she could see that it was a scrapbook. Just as she opened it, Mr. Stevenson appeared.

"What are you doing with that?" he barked.

Startled by his presence and his tone, Hope's hands jerked and a few pictures slid out of the book.

"I'm sorry," she said, quickly reaching down to pick up the pictures. But Mr. Stevenson had already snatched them up.

"This is private," he said gruffly. The old man took the book away from Hope and sank down on the couch. He ran his fingers across the cover, and a deep sadness filled his eyes.

"I didn't mean to upset you," Hope said gently. "Are they pictures of your family?"

Mr. Stevenson studied her for a long moment before nodding, "Once, yes."

He opened the book and Hope slid closer to him. They thumbed through several pages in silence.

"This was going to be our house," he said, pointing to a picture of the frame of a house. "My best friend was helping me build it." He smiled and chuckled a little as if recalling a funny moment.

With a sigh he turned the page and trailed his fingertip across the photo of a young woman. "This was my wife," he murmured. "I was building the house because she was pregnant. We were going to have a baby, a family." He shook his head as a rush of sorrow filled him. "Then everything changed."

He pointed to a picture of a group of men in Air Force uniforms, all quite young and handsome. "These were my Air Force pals; more like brothers really."

He tightened his lips for a moment and then cleared his throat. "With everything that happened, the stress was too much for the pregnancy, and the baby was never born. I never finished building that house, and I haven't heard from my friends or Air Force brothers in decades." He snapped the book shut and ran his hand over the cover again.

"I'm sorry if this brought up bad memories," Hope whispered.

Mr. Stevenson shook his head and looked at her with a hint of joy in his eyes. "Oh no, Hope, these are the good memories. They've kept me going all these years. Yes, it ended in sadness. But at one time, my life was much different." His voice trailed off.

Then he reached into his pocket. "This is for you," he said, awkwardly thrusting a wood carving at Hope. It was a perfect replica of Tango, and the girl could tell from the exquisite detail that Mr. Stevenson had worked on it for hours.

Hope was awestruck. "It's beautiful. Thank you."

"Go now," Mr. Stevenson commanded, his brusque nature returning. "Tomorrow, you can bring Tango to his new home."

Chapter Fourteen

How to Say Goodbye

Early the next morning Hope stood at the edge of the woods. She had been given permission to ride Tango to Mr. Stevenson's property and could not wait to see him. She whistled for him, and right away he came trotting up, as if he had been waiting.

"Oh, Tango!" Hope cried out. She stroked his coat and gently hugged his neck, then climbed up onto his back. Holding on tightly, she and Tango sped across the plains to catch up with the herd. Surrounded by the freedom of the wild horses, with the sounds of their hooves filling the air, and the same wind rushing through her hair that was streaming through their manes, Hope felt as if she belonged.

She could feel Tango's heart pounding, his body filling with the freedom of the open plains. When he finally slowed, the other horses in the herd dispersed to graze on what little grass was available.

"Tango, I found a home for you," Hope said quietly, even though, in glancing at the other horses, she knew Tango was already home. "It's a safe place, where you will be well cared for, and I'll be able to see you every day."

She guided him toward the mountain trail. Tango moved easily, as if he already knew where she wanted him to go. Soon the two were following the trail up the mountain to Mr. Stevenson's home.

The old man was waiting by the paddock gate when they arrived. Hope led Tango into the paddock, and at first he neighed and snorted at the unfamiliar surroundings. But soon he was grazing heavily on the lush grass.

"It's for the best," Mr. Stevenson assured her.

In the distance they heard the neighs of the other wild horses calling for Tango. Tango lifted his head in the direction of the sound. For a moment his muscles tensed as if he might run, then he lowered his head back to the grass.

"I hope so," the girl said with a frown.

Hope had expected to feel happier. She finally had what she wanted. Tango was safe, and she could see him as often as she liked. Yet watching Tango wander around the paddock, she couldn't help thinking, *but maybe it's not what he wants.* Having experienced the freedom he was used to, it felt wrong to see him behind a fence.

Later that night, listening to the shrill cries of the other horses of his herd, Tango snorted and snuffed against the ground. They were worried about him.

He neighed back loudly, but they could not hear him. They were searching for him. Sensing their fear, his heart pounded.

It was very dark, and he could hear the dogs barking in response to the cries of the horses. Tango had to go to them. He had to find them. He ran as fast as he could in wild circles, searching for a way out.

The next day Mr. Stevenson told Hope about all the noise Tango had made overnight. Together they went to the paddock and found Tango neighing wildly. He was bucking and charging at the gate of the paddock, turning just before he would crash into it.

Realizing what a terrible mistake she had made, Hope's heart sank. Tango didn't belong in a paddock, and he didn't belong with her. Yes, he loved her, she had no doubts about that, but she couldn't expect him to not want to be free.

Mr. Stevenson tried to reassure her. "He'll calm down. He just needs to get used to it."

Over the next few weeks, the girl hoped each day to hear that Tango had settled at night. But each day Mr. Stevenson told her the truth; Tango had been just as wild. The horse became so distracted he would not let Hope ride him and no longer responded to her soothing tones.

One afternoon, as Hope and Mr. Stevenson watched Tango pace the paddock, Hope realized there was nothing left to try.

Tango's eyes were wild with desperation, much like they were when she first met him. She knew Tango better than anyone else. She knew he was not happy.

Hope reached up to try to touch his mane, but he bucked and neighed in a way that almost frightened her. "I have to let him go," she said sadly.

"That's a decision only you can make," Mr. Stevenson said. He turned and walked away from the paddock, leaving Hope alone with Tango, who was demonstrating how wild he was.

Hope knew that if she did not let him out, Tango might hurt himself trying to get free. With tears in her eyes, she opened the gate. Tango rushed past her without hesitation, and she was certain he had made his choice.

Just before he disappeared into the woods, he paused and glanced back at Hope. Then he neighed loudly and bounded off, following the calls of his herd.

Hope could only stare after him. In the low tones she used to soothe him, she whispered to the breeze, hoping her words would reach him. "I will never forget you, Tango."

With the wind rushing through the trees on the mountain, Tango led the herd to a small pond. He listened for a familiar whistle, his ears perking and twitching. But it never came.

Tango and the herd drank deeply from the pond. Then they moved on toward the plains, breaking into a swift run. Even though he felt gloriously free, with the sky above him and the ground moving rapidly beneath his hooves, Tango sensed something was missing.

Nearing the edge of the woods, he expected to see Hope standing there, whistling. Yet no one was there, waiting for him.

The horses raced across the plains, their hooves kicking up a cloud of dust around their bodies, until they disappeared into the woods. They climbed carefully back up the mountainous trails to the area that was lush with grass.

Tango nickered quietly. The other horses nickered in return and watched as he turned away from them and made his way along the mountain trail.

He passed through the trees until he reached a familiar place. Standing at the edge of the property, he could see a young girl and an old man talking beside the paddock they had built for him. He ran toward them as quickly as he could.

Hope stood at the still open gate. When she heard the sound of hooves striking the ground, she looked up with tear-stained cheeks. "Tango!" Hope shrieked when he rushed right past her, through the gate and into the paddock.

The mustang trotted around the circular pen and shook his mane, as if to say, 'I am home.'

Hope had tears in her eyes when he walked up to her and nickered beside her. "Oh, Tango," she murmured, pressing her head against his, "I'm so glad you came back."

Tango nuzzled her neck in response. With Hope for a friend, he knew he would always be free.

Did You Enjoy This Book?

Dear Kind Reader,

*If you enjoyed **Hope's Horse: The Mystery of Shadow Ridge** and would like to help me reach more parents and kids with this book, please take a moment to write a review on Amazon. Your review makes a real difference, and I'd appreciate it very much.*

Thanks in advance!

With love,

Strawberry Shakespeare

About the Author

Strawberry Shakespeare was born and educated in New York City where she received a master's degree and doctoral training in clinical psychology. While working in the mental health field, she returned to her original love – writing – and is now a bestselling children's author and screenwriter.

Saving Bluestone Belle, Shakespeare's debut novel, is a popular children's book for ages 8-12, and has been a book club selection, a featured attraction and an award winner at book groups, book fairs, book festivals and animal rights conferences across the country. Her other bestselling children's books include *The Cloud Horse & Other Stories* and *Hope's Horse: The Mystery of Shadow Ridge.*

Shakespeare was interviewed by reporters at the Animal Rights National Conference in Los Angeles. What follows is a quote from that interview.

"How we treat the least among us is an indication of who we really are as a culture. Too often, horses are viewed as a disposable commodity rather than as faithful companions and helpmates of man. I was horrified by reports of their rampant abuse and exploitation by the horse slaughter industry, and decided to highlight this issue in my children's books. My hope is that this story will inspire young people to take a stand against cruelty toward horses and other animals."

Please read on to discover more books by Strawberry Shakespeare that your child is sure to love.

Children's Books by Strawberry Shakespeare

Saving Bluestone Belle

If your horse-loving kid enjoyed *Hope's Horse: The Mystery of Shadow Ridge,* you can be certain they will absolutely adore *Saving Bluestone Belle* by bestselling children's author Strawberry Shakespeare. This teacher-approved, award-winning comic-adventure is guaranteed to make your child laugh out loud and keep turning the pages with breathless excitement.

Saving Bluestone Belle tells about a stolen white horse and the ten-year-old boy who hits the road to rescue her. Along the way, young Homer goes up against an evil rancher and his wacky henchmen, only to be held captive in an underground fortress where he must use his quirky ingenuity to escape before it is too late!

This Disney-style story has been a featured attraction at children's book clubs, book fairs, book festivals and animal rights conferences across the country. It teaches children to be true to themselves and to care for the vulnerable creatures among us. Both avid and reluctant readers, boys and girls alike, will love the emphasis on snappy dialogue and fast-moving, action-oriented narrative.

The second edition of this popular book has been updated and enhanced by two additional interior illustrations, bringing the total number of original works by the talented contemporary artist, Mike Bilz, to 12. With its rollicking tale and delightful art, *Saving Bluestone Belle* is certain to thoroughly entertain the horse kids among you as well as the entire family.

Saving Bluestone Belle is a 154 page novel for ages 8-12. The new second edition is available on Amazon in two formats: Kindle and paperback. The first edition hardcover collectible is also available on Amazon and BarnesandNoble.com.

The Cloud Horse & Other Stories

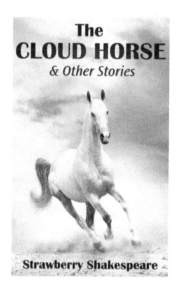

Your horse kids ages 8-12 will also love *The Cloud Horse & Other Stories* by Strawberry Shakespeare and C. J. Dennis. This delightful volume contains three unforgettable and uplifting stories for children.

Boys and girls who can't get enough of horses and adventure will adore the title story, "The Cloud Horse," an exhilarating yarn about a kid who is whisked away on the back of a flying horse!

Based on "The Boy Who Rode into the Sunset," by Australian author C. J. Dennis, this classic tale is a personal favorite of children's author Strawberry

Shakespeare. In her quest to bring it to modern audiences, she made several valuable enhancements to the original. These include creating an evocative new story title, designing a beautiful book cover, dividing the story into colorfully-named chapters and penning a fascinating chapter on the life and times of C. J. Dennis, all of which render this magical fable more meaningful and enjoyable than ever.

This volume also contains "White Fire" and "The Appaloosa Colt," two extraordinary short stories by bestselling children's author Strawberry Shakespeare. Readers of all ages will be enchanted by these mystical and inspiring tales.

The ebook and paperback editions of The *Cloud Horse & Other Stories* are available on Amazon.com. The ebook edition is also available on BarnesandNoble.com.

Hope's Horse: The Mystery of Shadow Ridge

In this exciting novel by Strawberry Shakespeare, a 12-year-old girl, accompanied by the wild mustang she calls a friend, is drawn into a decades-old mystery surrounding the scary 'man on the mountain' and a strange metallic object buried in the woods.

Hope's Horse: The Mystery of Shadow Ridge, by best-selling children's author Strawberry Shakespeare, is a riveting, horse-themed mystery-adventure tale for young readers ages 9-12. Set in the California Eastern Sierras, it tells the story of twelve-year-old Hope Miller and her wild mustang, Tango.

While recovering from the death of her beloved grandfather, who shared her love of horses, Hope is forbidden by her parents to go on the mountain alone or anywhere near the wild horses she adores. So the girl keeps her horse, Tango, a secret from her parents, and rides him on the mountain without their knowledge.

On one of these outings, she and Tango evade evil poachers only to encounter a scary old mountain man. Escaping in a mad dash up the dark side of the mountain, they discover a mysterious metal object buried on Shadow Ridge. Hope instinctively knows her find is important and that she should tell her parents about it. But if she tells, she would also have to reveal the truth about her and Tango, and would probably never see him again.

A surprising turn of events merges the destinies of Hope, Tango and the old man on the mountain during a dramatic confrontation with dangerous horse poachers. The resulting explosion of action, excitement, heartache and, ultimately, joyous healing is a must-read experience for the whole family and for every kid who loves mystery, adventure and horse stories.

Hope's Horse: The Mystery of Shadow Ridge is available on Amazon in print and Kindle editions. It is also available at BarnesandNoble.com.

All of the children's horse books by Strawberry Shakespeare make perfect gifts for young readers. Order them now. Kids treasure these bestselling tales and so will you!

Free Gift

The Reading Advantage

Quick & Easy Ways to Transform Your Child into a Passionate Reader!

As my thanks to all the wonderful parents, grandparents and teachers who have read *Hope's Horse: The Mystery of Shadow Ridge,* I would like you to have the bonus ebook, *The Reading Advantage: Quick & Easy Ways to Transform Your Child into a Passionate Reader!* Written by psychologist/author Strawberry Shakespeare, this ebook provides powerful techniques that will not only increase your child's interest in reading but will also bring you and your child closer.

The research proves that avid readers have an advantage in life. Now you can give your child the same reading advantage.

Visit https://bit.ly/TheReadingAdvantage to download your free gift.

Made in the USA
Middletown, DE
19 May 2020